THE QUEST FOR CRESTS

DIGITAL DIGIMON MONSTERS ™

J.E. Bright

HarperEntertainment
An Imprint of HarperCollinsPublishers

HarperEntertainment
An Imprint of HarperCollins*Publishers*
10 East 53rd Street, New York, NY 10022-5299

HarperCollins books are available at special quantity discounts for bulk purchases for sales promotions, premiums, or fund-raising. For information please call or write: Special Markets Department, HarperCollins Publishers Inc., 10 East 53rd Street, New York, NY 10022-5299. Telephone: (212) 207-7528. Fax: (212) 207-7222.

ISBN 0-06-107199-4

First printing: March 2001

Printed in the United States of America

Visit HarperEntertainment on the World Wide Web at
www.harpercollins.com

❖ 10 9 8 7 6 5 4 3 2 1

Part One:
Server Bound!

1

A pillar of rainbow light appeared on the beach of File Island.

Fresh from their victorious battle with evil Devimon, the Digidestined kids and their Digimon friends marveled at the swirling colors of the brilliant column.

Then they gasped as a mysterious being materialized inside the stream of light, floating five feet off the ground.

The ancient man wasn't taller than second-grader Takeru "T.K." Takaishi. His eyes were closed and he smiled contentedly as he hovered in the rainbow pillar. His sneakers were extremely large.

"So, you children are the Digidestined," the mysterious man said. His voice was calm, although deep and gravelly. "You must be strong to have defeated Devimon."

Taichi Kamiya, better known as Tai, stepped closer to the pillar. "Who are you?"

"Are you a friend of Devimon's?" Yamato "Matt" Ishida asked.

The man in the pillar smiled. "Fear not, for I am a friend to all," he replied. "And yet . . . I am a friend to none."

Sora Takenouchi adjusted her blue hat. "I can't believe it," she said. "There are actually other humans besides us in this world!"

"I am human," the floating old man told her. "And yet . . . I am not human. My name is

Gennai." He bowed inside the rainbow pillar. "I couldn't send you this transmission during your battle with Devimon. But now the lines are clear and only ten cents a minute!"

"Where are you?" Koushiro "Izzy" Izumi asked. Izzy's laptop computer was hanging from a strap on his back.

"I am speaking to you from across the ocean," Gennai answered. "I am on the Continent of Server."

"Talk about a long-distance call!" Sora exclaimed. "How long have you been there?"

"Since before the beginning," Gennai replied, "and until after the end."

A confused look crossed Mimi Tachikawa's pretty face. "Are you the one who got us stuck here in the Digital World?" she asked.

"It was not I," Gennai replied.

"Then, who was it?" Mimi chirped.

Gennai remained silent for a long moment. "It was—" he began.

The kids and their Digimon friends leaned forward in anticipation. That question had been on their minds since they'd been transported to File Island in what seemed such a long time ago.

"I don't know," Gennai finished.

Everyone let out a disappointed groan.

T.K. peered up at the mysterious man. "But, Mr. Gennai, sir," he asked, "do you know what we need to do to get back home again?"

"No, I don't," Gennai replied cheerfully.

Tai squinted at Gennai. "Boy, you're a regular fountain of information," he said sarcastically.

"I'm sorry I can't help you," Gennai said, "but you can be of help to me." Gennai waited for the friends' mutters of amazed disbelief to settle down before he continued. "Please come to Server and defeat our enemies," he pleaded. "As you are the Digidestined, I have faith in you."

"That's crazy," Izzy complained. "We don't even know your exact location."

"Good point," Gennai said. "I forgot you're from out of town. Let me create a map for you on your computer." He blinked once, and a haze of purple light misted around Izzy's laptop.

"What if your enemies are humungazoid?" Joe Kido asked Gennai nervously, pushing up his glasses. "Do you think we can beat anything tougher than Devimon?"

"Not yet," Gennai replied, "but if your Digimon can digivolve once more, you might be able to do it."

Agumon, Tai's Digimon pal, had an astounded look on his face. "You mean we can digivolve even more?"

Gennai nodded. "Yes, but you'll need these in order to do it." The old man vanished inside the pillar, and in his place appeared a small device that looked like a luggage tag on a chain. Next to the tag, a small gold card materialized.

As the objects glowed,

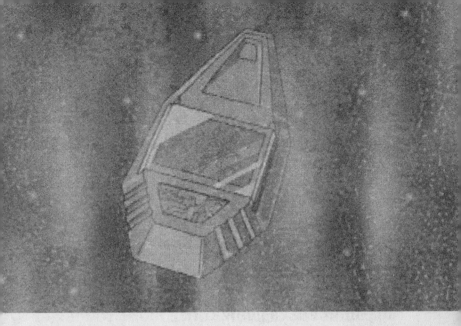

Gennai's voice could still be heard. "If you have the tags and crests," he said, "your Digimon will be able to digivolve even further."

"Please tell us where we can find these tags and crests," Gabumon begged. Gabumon sort of resembled a striped hamster with a horn on its head.

The tags and crests flashed again, and then faded out. They were quickly replaced by the image of Gennai. "Well, the crests are scattered about," the ancient man said. "You can locate them all throughout the Continent of

Server. And the tags were secretly sealed away somewhere by Devimon."

Before Gennai could tell them anything else, the rainbow pillar began crackling with static.

"Is something wrong?" Sora asked.

"Oh, no!" Gennai cried as his picture flickered. "Devimon–oh, no! You must come . . . ahh!"

Matt stared at the sputtering pillar in alarm. "What's going on?"

"Ahhh!" Gennai moaned. "Come . . . quickly!" he pleaded. "I'll be waiting! On Server–"

The pillar of rainbow light winked out.

"He's gone," Tai said.

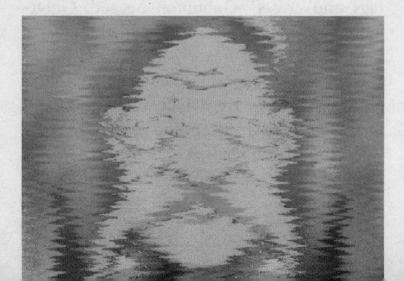

2

Tentomon buzzed his beetle's wings as he landed next to Izzy. "Gennai's transmission ended rather abruptly," he droned.

Izzy opened his laptop. "Well, at least he was able to send the map through before he got cut off," he replied. He checked out the diagram on the screen. It was green and blue, and showed a curving coastline.

"I hope Gennai's all right," Sora said. "What's our next move going to be?"

Tai balled up his fists in a fighting pose. "I've got a foolproof plan," he declared.

Then Tai relaxed his hands and smiled. "First we'll eat something," he joked. "And after that, I'm open to suggestions!"

The friends built a crackling campfire on the sandy shore while the sunset glimmered on the ocean. The stars rose above the surrounding palm trees. Gomamon popped out of the water with the main dish—a tasty fish he'd caught in his mouth. He smiled proudly as he paddled toward the gang waiting to eat.

They stuffed their faces with berries, fish, and a few delicious roots Palmon dug up. By the time the food was gone, the kids and Digimon were full . . . and sleepy.

A few minutes later, a shooting star split the night.

But none of the friends saw it. They were already snoring happily.

In the morning, T.K. woke up first. He carefully carried his Digi-egg to the edge of the woods. T.K.'s Digimon, Patamon, had finally learned to digivolve only a few days ago, just in time to face Devimon. Patamon had transformed into Angemon, a radiant warrior spirit. Angemon's power had been strong enough to defeat Devimon completely. But the effort had used up all of his energy. Angemon had returned to being an egg.

T.K. sat on a tree stump and sadly rubbed the Digi-egg, missing Patamon.

"T.K.?" Matt whispered sleepily as he wandered over.

"Oh," T.K. whimpered, "I was just wishing my Digi-egg would hurry up and hatch already so it could grow up."

"Don't sweat it, little bro," Matt said, tousling T.K.'s hair. "When your Digimon

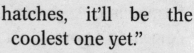

hatches, it'll be the coolest one yet."

T.K. hopped off the stump, grinning. "Egg-*zactly!*" he cheered.

Near the campfire, Tai jumped to his feet the moment he opened his eyes. "Okay!" he announced. "Now that we've gotten a good night's sleep, what are we going to do next?"

"You know what's next," Sora told him. She brushed pine needles and sand off her pants. "We have to go to Server to save Gennai from his enemies."

Izzy pulled up Gennai's map on his laptop. "Well, according to my calculations of longitude and latitude," he said, "I'd say Server is . . . pretty far away."

Mimi rested her chin in her hands. "I can't even swim across the bathtub, let alone an ocean," she whined. "I'll never make it."

Joe cleared his throat at the head of the campfire circle. "Why do we have to go?" he

asked. "Devimon's gone from the island. The Black Gears have disappeared, too. We wouldn't have to worry about food or water—"

"What are you saying?" Sora broke in.

Joe raised his palms nervously. "Why should we believe what this weirdo Gennai guy says?" he asked. "How do we know that Server really exists?"

Tai jumped in front of Joe. "If we hang around here, guys," he argued, "we'll never get back home."

"I don't know," Sora said. She looked down worriedly at her feet. Biyomon, a pink parakeet-like Digimon, peered at her sympathetically. "Devimon almost got us!" Sora reminded everybody. "Maybe we shouldn't go. At least we know what we're up against here."

Izzy closed his laptop with a click. "Even if we wanted to go," he added, "what mode of transportation would we utilize?"

"We don't even know what the fashions are like on Server!" piped Mimi.

Joe nodded at Mimi's statement as if it proved his point.

"Maybe we *should* stay here a while longer," Matt said, "and think this through."

Tai became riled as his friends suggested staying. Matt was the last straw. "What's with you, man?" Tai demanded angrily.

Before Tai could start a fight, T.K. hopped to his feet. "Let's go!" he declared.

Everybody gazed at T.K. in amazement.

T.K. put his hands on his hips. "We don't know what kind of danger is out there," he said, "but let's find out! I'm sure Angemon would say the same thing if he were still here. So . . . I'm going!"

"We'll go, too!" Agumon announced. He stepped into the circle. "If we have the tags and crests, we'll be able to digivolve again, right? Once we transform into our new shapes, we'll be able to protect you for sure."

"You da mon!" Tai cheered.

Mimi pressed her big, pink cowboy hat firmly onto her head. "Well, I'm not staying by myself," she said cheerfully. "I'll go, too!"

Even Joe had to give in. He smiled and pushed up his glasses. "Okay, I'm convinced."

"Then it's unanimous!" Izzy exclaimed.

Tai raised his fists into the air. "We're going to Server!"

3

Agumon stomped toward the forest to start making a raft. "Pepper Breath!" he hollered. A fireball burst from Agumon's mouth and slammed into a pine tree's trunk. The tree toppled toward the beach.

"Timber!" Tai cried, jumping back. The tree crashed on the sand in front of him.

"Blue Blaster!" Gabumon shouted, sending a stream of sizzling blue electricity into the woods. The other Digimon had to run out of the way as Gabumon's blast felled another tree.

Watching from the side with Sora, Izzy sighed. "At our current rate," he calculated, "it'll take *forever* to build a raft."

"Don't worry about it, Izzy," Sora replied calmly. "It's not like we're in any kind of hurry–"

The sound of heavy footsteps caught Sora's attention. She wheeled around and saw a monster heading her way. He had a cat's head and an imposing, muscular giant man's body. Sora let out a piercing scream.

Izzy stood up. "Leomon!" he yelled.

Even though Leomon had eventually helped save the kids, he'd also tried to destroy them while brainwashed by Devimon. He had a scowl on his face as he stalked closer.

Sora and Izzy backed away.

"So, I heard you're going to Server," Leomon growled. The dangling earring in his left ear glinted.

Sora bravely faced Leomon. "How did you hear?" she asked with a gulp.

Leomon shrugged. "Oh, you know monsters," he said. "They love to gossip. I thought I'd see if you needed help with anything."

When they realized the monster was being friendly, Sora and Izzy laughed and rushed over to Leomon's side.

"You mean you'll really help us?" Sora asked.

With a smile, Leomon nodded. "I've got a few friends who want to help, too."

Digimon of all types began to emerge from the woods. First came Elecmon, who protected baby Digimon in the File Island nursery. Then Mojyamon and Centarumon stepped out of the forest.

Mojyamon resembled a furry ice troll, and Centarumon wore purple and orange armor on his half-horse–half-man body. They were followed by Monzaemon, a yellow teddy bear–like Digimon who ruled Toy Town, and Frigimon, a snowmanlike Digimon who lived in Freezeland. Finally, the fiery Meramon joined the others, with a pack of floral Yokomon at his feet.

The kids had rescued most of the monsters from Devimon's horrid Black Gears. The gang welcomed them with happy, laughing cheers.

Leomon got right to work. "Fist of the Beast King!" he shouted as he knocked trees down with his power punch.

The other Digimon helped Leomon with their own mighty attacks.

Wood exploded in midair as blasts splintered the huge trees. By the time the tide

went out that afternoon, the raft was ready. The strapped-together logs splashed into the ocean—and floated easily on the waves.

The raft had a white sail flapping merrily on a tall mast. Tied to the mast were barrels of supplies for the journey.

"It's hydrodynamically designed!" Izzy exclaimed.

Joe stared at the raft, his stomach churning. "I think I'm getting seasick already," he moaned.

"Get a grip, Joe," Tai scolded. "It'll have to do."

Leomon strode between the kids to the waterline. "Believe me," he promised, "that raft is strong enough to get you across the ocean."

Tai smiled at the muscular monster. "Leomon," he said, "we never could have done it without you."

"Oh!" T.K. shouted. Everyone glanced at him to see what was the matter.

The Digi-egg was trembling in T.K.'s hands!

T.K. inhaled sharply as a crack appeared

in the egg. He held his breath as the top split open.

A tiny, shapeless white blob with round black eyes smiled up at T.K. "Hi ya!" it peeped.

"My Digi-egg!" T.K. cried. "It hatched!"

"Poyo!" the tiny white blob squeaked. "Poyomon!"

Poyomon bounced out of the broken Digi-egg. T.K. grabbed him and hugged him tightly. The little blob giggled. "Yay!" T.K. sang. "He did it!"

Whirring his wings, Tentomon hovered

nearby. "Poyomon is a small Digimon of few words," the insectoid Digimon buzzed. "But if his friends are in trouble, he's ready for action!"

"We're ready, too!" Tai announced. "Everybody aboard!"

The kids and the Digimon hurried onto the raft. The wide sail filled with air, and they slowly cruised out toward the open ocean.

"This is good-bye!" Leomon called from shore. The other monsters surrounded him, waving farewell.

"Thanks!" Tai hollered back. "Good-bye!"

4

Tai peered at the watery horizon through his small spyglass. "I can't see anything," he reported. The raft had left all sight of land behind, with nothing but blue sea all around. The rippling tips of the waves twinkled in the brilliant sunlight.

"How much longer will this trip take?" Joe asked.

"Chill out," Tai replied. "We just left."

Joe let out a long sigh. "The salt air's killing my sinuses," he complained. "And we've only got enough food for two weeks."

Tai shrugged as he returned to scanning the horizon. "If we run out of food, we'll catch some fish."

"Well, this is beautiful weather for sailing," Sora said. She raised her face to the sunshine.

The waves rocking the boat suddenly got bigger. They rolled with power, swelling higher and wilder.

"Ugh!" Mimi cried. She swayed on the raft's deck. "I don't feel so good."

Izzy held on to a barrel. "I didn't calculate these waves being so rough."

Joe stared out over the water. "Did another boat cause these waves?" he asked.

"No boat can do that," Tai answered. His eyes widened as a humongous shape reared up out of the water. "An island!" he cried.

"An island?" Sora shot back. "Since when does an island have *fins*?"

26

They all screamed as the vast shape revealed itself to be an immense whale. He was ten times as big as the raft. The whale skimmed beneath the friends like a giant shadow under the water.

After he passed the raft, the whale lifted his gigantic tail into the air.

"Heads up!" Tai hollered.

The tail splashed beside the raft, dousing everybody with salty spray.

"It's Whamon," Tentomon buzzed nervously. "He's a giant Digimon who lives in the deep oceans of DigiWorld."

"He's massive!" Gabumon exclaimed.

Tentomon nodded. "A Whamon can sometimes be fierce," he stated. "But I've never seen one act *this* aggressive."

Whamon surfaced in front of the raft and opened his cavernous mouth. His teeth were each the size of one of the kids. Behind the teeth, the wide throat stretched like a pink subway tunnel into the depths of the whale.

"No, don't eat me!" Mimi screeched as the raft was sucked into Whamon's mouth. She clung to the mast, squeezing shut her eyes.

Whamon's huge jaws clamped down, closing them in blubbery darkness. The raft swirled down the vast tunnel.

"I hope we don't give him a sore throat!" Sora shouted.

"Technically, we're not in the throat anymore," Izzy explained as the boat sailed through the fleshy passageway. "We're in the esophagus, which leads to the stomach."

Joe shuddered. "He thinks we're fast food?"

Mimi peeked open her eyes and gasped. "So, he really did eat us!"

"Sooner or later," Sora said, "this has to lead to an exit."

With a grimace, Izzy nodded. "It does, but you don't want to go there!"

Then the tunnel suddenly ended. The raft launched into a vast open space, and every-

body hollered as the boat fell through the air. They plopped down on the calm surface of a stinky, greenish-blue lake, and drifted to a halt.

"Finally, we've stopped," Sora said with relief.

Joe peered at the curved pink walls around the lake and the slimy, rounded ceiling overhead. "Where are we?" he asked.

"According to anatomy," Izzy answered, "this would be the stomach."

"The stomach?" T.K. asked, hugging Poyomon closer to him. "Isn't that where food goes after it's chewed up?"

"Yeah," Matt replied. He sounded thoroughly grossed out.

Izzy pointed toward one wall, where mustard-yellow ooze was sliding down into the stomach's pool. "Gastric juice!" he screamed. Izzy broke out in a terrified sweat.

"What?" Mimi shrieked.

"It's the stuff in the stomach that dissolves the food!" Izzy answered. He backed up to the middle of the raft as the gastric juice seeped across the surface. When the yellow ooze touched the logs, the wood sizzled and hissed.

"We're melting!" T.K. cried.

Tai herded his friends toward the center of the raft. "Don't let it get on you!"

Sora grabbed Tai's arm, and pointed toward the stomach's ceiling. "Look up there!"

Tai glanced up. A spiky object was embedded in the flesh above. "It's a Black Gear!"

"That's why Whamon was acting so aggressive," Agumon explained.

"Poison Ivy!" Palmon shouted. Her vine arms stretched up to the ceiling, and she wrapped her leafy hands around the Black Gear's teeth. "Someone can climb up on these!" she offered.

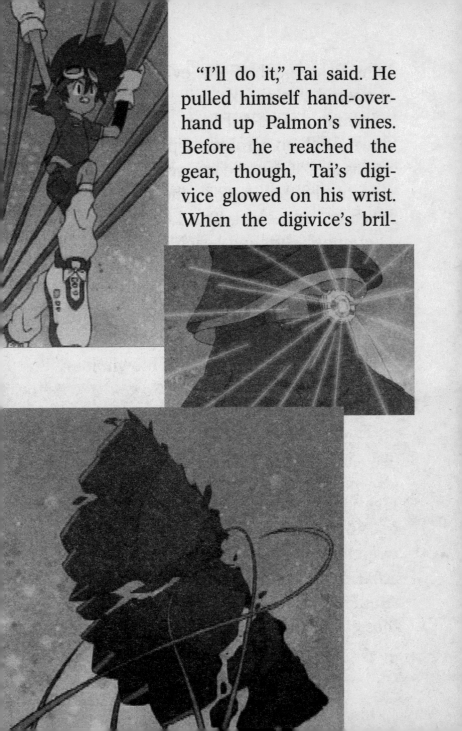

"I'll do it," Tai said. He pulled himself hand-over-hand up Palmon's vines. Before he reached the gear, though, Tai's digivice glowed on his wrist. When the digivice's brilliant light touched the evil Black Gear, it shattered into specks.

Palmon's arms fell loose, and Tai plunged down. With an acrobatic flip, he landed safely on his feet. "Okay, I destroyed it," Tai said.

Instantly, the water in the stomach began to churn and swirl. The kids and the little Digimons clutched each other. A hole stretched open in the ceiling, and everything in the stomach gushed up it.

Seconds later, the friends spurted into the sky far above Whamon.

He'd spouted them out his blowhole!

5

The force of the waterspout was too much for the battered raft. It split apart, and the timbers tumbled into the ocean around Whamon. The kids and Digimon plummeted into the cold sea.

In front of Mimi, Whamon opened his warehouse of a mouth.

"Go away!" Mimi shrieked. "Not again!"

"Sorry about that," Whamon said in a friendly, rumbling voice. "I must've had a tummy ache or something."

Biyomon waved a wing. "We know it wasn't your fault," she chirped.

"That's right," Sora added. "It was the Black Gear inside you."

Tai clung to a log beside Agumon. "Those Black Gears are rude!" he exclaimed. "I bet that's the last one."

"I bet you're wrong," Joe muttered. Gomamon, who was an excellent swimmer, held Joe afloat.

"Thanks, kids," Whamon said. "I owe you one!"

"Don't mention it," Tai replied. "It was our pleasure. By the way, do you know how far it is to Server?"

Mild waves rippled around Whamon. "Yes, it would take me about five days to swim to Server," he answered. "Make that three and a half without traffic. Are you going there?"

With a rueful laugh, Agumon gestured at the floating timbers. "We were trying to," he replied.

"I could use a change of scenery," Whamon said. "I'll take you there myself. It's not every day your lunch saves your life!"

Whamon sank so the kids and Digimon could wade onto his back. Once they were settled, he skimmed over the ocean, surging toward Server.

Tai faced the ocean breeze, which whipped his wild hair. "Now if we only knew where to find those tags and crests that Devimon hid somewhere."

"Did you say Devimon?" Whamon rumbled.

"Yeah," Tai replied. "Do you know him?"

"I don't know anything about tags or crests," Whamon said. "But a while ago, Devimon hid something deep at the bottom of the ocean."

"Can you tell us where?" Tai asked.

Whamon stopped. "It's on the way to

Server," he explained. "You can all ride inside me and I'll take you there. But no tickling!"

The friends climbed down and hurried into Whamon's open mouth. They hung out on his tongue as he sealed his lips together. Then Whamon dived deep beneath the sea, to the darkest depths of the ocean. On the bottom, Whamon glided between stone caverns and found a cave filled with a huge air bubble.

At the cave's entrance, Whamon let the kids and the Digimon out. "I have to rest here," the whale said wearily. "I am *so* out of shape. I've got to drop a couple thousand pounds."

"Thanks, Whamon," Tai said, when he had his feet back on solid rock. Whamon swam away, disappearing in the maze of rock canyons on the ocean floor.

Inside the cave, the friends followed a series of stone tunnels. Down a narrow passageway, they discovered a gleaming shop in a cavern. "What's that?" Joe asked.

"It's a convenience store!" Tai replied.

But before Tai could take two steps toward the undersea mini-mart, the ground split open in front of him. He jumped back as a giant mole like Digimon with a drill on its head burrowed up.

"Drimogemon!" Tentomon exclaimed. "He lives deep inside the earth drilling tunnels, and uses his Iron Drill Spin and Crusher Bone to wipe out his enemies."

Drimogemon was fat and fuzzy, with white and purple fur. His huge paws ended in sharp claws. He growled, and the friends could see a Black Gear stuck in his forehead!

Joe groaned. "I knew Whamon's wasn't the last one," he muttered.

Drimogemon reared up out of his hole and raised his rock-cutting claws. "It is Lord Devimon's will that no one shall pass!" he shouted. The horn on Drimogemon's head spun faster with a dentist-drill whine.

"You think that drill scares us?" Gomamon jeered. "Think again." The rookie Digimon raised his soft flippers, and shouted, "Gomamon, digivolve into . . . Ikkakumon!"

Instantly, the cave exploded with swirls of digital information. Electricity sizzled around Gomamon as he swelled in size. He had looked like a white baby seal with a Mohawk haircut, but now he transformed into a giant, hairy walruslike Digimon with

a pointy horn on his head. Ikkakumon roared as he charged the big molelike Digimon.

"Drill Spin!" Drimogemon hollered as his horn clashed with Ikkakumon's. They slammed their horns together like expert sword fighters.

"Now's our chance!" Tai cried. He dashed toward the convenience store, followed by his friends.

They were only in the store for a second before Ikkakumon bashed Drimogemon so hard that he crashed through the big front window.

"Harpoon Torpedo!" Ikkakumon bellowed. His horn launched like a missile—and exploded on Drimogemon's chest. The store filled with dust and smoke.

Then Tentomon swooped toward Drimo-

gemon. "Tentomon digivolve into . . . Kabuterimon!" he screeched.

Tentomon had looked like a big june bug
with a nervous expression, but as digital
energy swirled around him, he changed into
a seven-foot-tall alien wasplike Digimon.

"Crusher Bone!" Drimogemon shouted.
Instantly, a long white bone whirled
through the air at Kabuterimon, but the
digivolved Champion soared right over it.

Kabuterimon aimed carefully at the gear.

"Electro Shocker!" he yowled. A current of green energy coursed out of Kabuterimon's eyes and zapped into the Black Gear. It fried, crumbling to dust.

Drimogemon toppled over onto his side, knocked out.

As the dust settled, T.K. realized he hadn't seen Poyomon for a few minutes. He frantically searched the smoky store. "Poyomon! Where are you?"

"Poyo!" came a distant reply. T.K. followed the voice. "Poyo!"

In a storage room, T.K. found Poyomon near a bunch of crates. Poyomon was clinging to a small, maroon box.

"What's in that?" T.K. asked.

"Poyo!" Poyomon replied.

Back in the store's main room, Drimogemon woke up. "Please forgive me for attacking you," he begged sheepishly.

T.K. and Poyomon hurried into the main room. The maroon box was open in T.K.'s hands, and seven golden objects sparkled dazzlingly inside it.

43

"The tags!" Matt exclaimed. Each tag resembled a luggage nameplate, with a glowing gem in its center.

Izzy nodded. "Just like the ones Gennai showed us during his transmission."

"How pretty!" Mimi added.

"Remember what Gennai told us," Matt said. He picked up a tag and hung it around his neck. "The crests are scattered throughout the Continent of Server."

"Yeah," Gabumon said, "if we get both the tags and the crests—"

"We'll all be able to digivolve once again!" Agumon finished for him.

"Then we'll just have to find the crests!" Tai declared.

Part Two: Etemon's Dark Network

6

Tai stood lookout at dawn while his friends slept. His shoes were firmly planted on top of Whamon's rubbery, enormous head—hundreds of feet above the water.

For the past four days, Whamon took the friends on a leisurely cruise across the sparkling ocean. Mainly everybody just kicked back and enjoyed the ride.

Now, however, Tai and the others were anxious to get to Server.

"I think I see an iceberg!" Tai exclaimed, peering through his spyglass. A gleaming white mass appeared on the horizon. "It's either that or the Continent of Server."

"It's Server," Whamon confirmed.

Tai strode over to his sleeping friends. "Rise and shine!" he hollered. "Land ho!" He gave Matt a shake. "C'mon, we're going to be there in a few minutes!"

Whamon sailed into a long lagoon surrounded by jagged stone sea stacks. They arrived at a cliff that was about ten feet shorter than Whamon. Tai and Agumon immediately jumped ashore. The other kids and Digimons slid to the ground until only Mimi was left up on Whamon's head.

"Uh, this is a little too extreme sports for me," Mimi whined as she peered down the high slope of blubber. "Is there some way I can be airlifted onto the island?"

Joe cupped his hands around his mouth like a megaphone. "Just put one foot in front of the other," he called. "It's as easy as

falling off a log!"

"I've fallen off plenty of logs," Mimi called back. "It's not as easy as it looks!" Whamon twitched, and Mimi lost her balance, sliding down to the shore. She crashed into Joe. "I broke a nail!" Mimi complained.

Whamon slowly turned around in the lagoon. "Good luck finding the crests!"

The kids waved and called out their thanks as the whalelike Digimon swam away. Whamon flipped his tail in the air, diving into the deep.

"So, what are we going to do now?" Mimi asked.

Palmon pointed inland with one of her leafy arms. "Whamon told us that there's a Koromon village in the forest a few miles from here."

"Koromon?" Mimi asked. "That sounds familiar."

Agumon nudged Mimi with his mini-dinosaur snout. "I was a Koromon the day you got here!" he exclaimed. "Before I digivolved."

"I forgot!" Mimi chirped.

Tai strode away from the shoreline. "Okay, gang, let's move out!" he called over his shoulder.

For the next few hours, the friends marched across a rocky desert that had very few shade trees. The sun beat down mercilessly as they trudged through the barren land.

"I'd give anything to be in a nice clean bathtub with lots of bubbles," Mimi said, fanning herself with her big hat.

Palmon glanced at her. "You can do that once we get to the village."

"You honestly think they have bathtubs, Palmon?" Mimi asked, her voice full of hope.

Palmon shrugged. She didn't seem sure at all.

Agumon stopped and began

to sniff the air. "I smell Koromon!" he announced.

Tai took a look through his spyglass. In the distance, he spotted a patch of dark green between two hills. "I see a forest!"

"Is that where the Koromon village is?" Matt asked.

Tai started to run toward the hills. "It must be!" he called back.

Everybody hurried after Tai across the hot sands, and soon they reached the woods. When the friends stepped into the shade of the thick vines overhead, the air felt much cooler. Mimi sighed in relief.

The gang followed a path through the forest, climbing up a gentle, tree-furred hill. When they reached the top, a small village appeared below, spread out in a valley. The buildings were cloth huts that looked like mushrooms. In the middle of town, a tall tower loomed.

"Great!" T.K. cheered. "We can rest!"

Mimi clasped her hands to her chest. "Even better," she squealed, "I can take a bath!" Mimi took off toward the village.

"Wait!" Palmon cried, chasing after her. "Stop!"

"A bath!" Mimi hollered as she raced through the dirt streets. "Somebody grab me a rubber ducky!"

Mimi screeched to a halt when she saw a group of little round blobs with no legs staring at her. There were dozens of the teeny pink critters. Each of them had two wings on heads where a human's ears would be. "Excuse me," Mimi asked politely, "where's the shampoo?"

The blobs blinked at her with their orange eyes and smiled.

Palmon arrived next to Mimi. "Do you really think that these are Koromon?" Mimi asked.

"No way," Palmon replied. "These are Pagumon. And there's more to them than meets the eye."

Giggles swept across the group of Pagumon. They waved their wings in amusement.

Then they rushed at Palmon, knocking her down. The Pagumons grabbed Mimi with their wings. They carried her away like a rowdy rock-concert crowd passing around a stage diver.

Mimi screamed.

7

Palmon jumped to her feet and chased after the Pagumon. "They've got Mimi!" she cried.

The other kids and Digimon ran after her toward the tower. "Don't let 'em get away!" Joe shouted. The huts weren't taller than Joe, but the tower rose higher than the surrounding forest.

The friends halted at the base of the lofty, skinny tent. Waiting in front of the tower's door flap were bunches of Pagumon. They smiled.

"Where is she?" Tai hollered.

The Pagumon just smiled some more.

"Help!" Mimi's voice shrieked from high above.

"In the tower–!" Tai shouted. He strode through the clusters of Pagumon and hurried inside. When his friends joined him, they found themselves inside a sheik's tent. Thick drapes dangled along glittering ruby walls. The floors glinted like rose-colored marble, and two curving stairways led to the upper levels.

T.K. pointed to a pink cowboy hat on the stairs. "Look, that's Mimi's hat!"

Sora hurried up the steps and examined it. "It's Mimi's," she said. "It's still got the price tag."

The kids ran up to the second-floor landing. Airy curtains made the space look like a sultan's throne room. In a nearby hallway, a pink pocketbook lay on the floor.

"That's Mimi's purse," Joe said. "She never goes anywhere without it!"

"Logically, that could only mean one thing," Izzy stated. "She's missing!"

Tai and Izzy rushed down the corridor, heading for a curtained doorway at the other end.

Meanwhile, Sora noticed a laundry basket on a shelf in the hall. A pink sleeve stuck out of the basket. Sora immediately yelled,

"No, Tai! Don't go in there!"

But Tai had already parted the curtain. "Mimi!" he shouted.

As Tai entered the steamy room with Izzy right behind him, the clouds cleared. Mimi was sitting in a bathtub with her back to the door. One of her bare legs stuck out of the water. Mimi hummed to herself happily.

"Mimi! Sorry!" Izzy gasped.

With a shriek, Mimi turned her wet head. She blushed deep red when she saw the boys. "Have either of you ever heard the phrase, 'Please knock before entering'?"

Tai and Izzy blushed, too. "Mimi," Tai

explained awkwardly, "we're here to rescue you and–"

Mimi hurled a metal bowl at him. She nailed Izzy with a heavy bottle of shampoo. Both boys fell backward onto the hallway floor.

"I told you not to go in," Sora reminded the boys. She closed the curtain, blocking Mimi from sight.

Tai and Izzy didn't reply–they were too busy nursing their sore noggins.

As night fell in the village, the Pagumon led the friends to a wide room on the top floor of the tall tower. The room was fancily decorated with heavy yellow curtains and comfy cushions, all bathed in golden light. The kids and the Digimon sat down and watched the Pagumon singing and dancing while they served a feast.

Welcome to our village,
we hope you never go!
Stay and visit with us,
and please enjoy the show!

The little pinkish creatures wore party hats. Some clapped their wings together, while others passed around bowls of fruits and vegetables. They all hopped like bouncing kickballs as they chanted.

We're here to entertain you—
we like to make you laugh!
And if you want to sign a check,
we'll take your autograph!

That fruit that you've been eating,
it's really ripe and sweet.
But guess what: when we picked it,
we only used our feet!

"This is *definitely* a Pagumon village," Gabumon groaned.

Agumon plucked a banana out of a bowl. "Something's wrong here, Gabumon," he whispered. "I know what I smelled were Koromon. I'd bet my nose on it!"

Across the room, T.K. held Poyomon, who was chewing an apple. The baby Digimon's eyes were closed in contentment. "You like that?" T.K. asked.

Poyomon nodded and swallowed. His eyes suddenly popped open wide with surprise. "Poyomon digivolve into . . . Tokomon!" he squealed. The baby Digimon exploded with light so brilliant that the entire room suddenly seemed to be in black and white. He had looked like a small, colorless blob, but now he grew a little bigger, with long, sleek ears and stubby legs.

"Hey, he's Tokomon again!" T.K. cheered.

Tokomon hopped into T.K.'s arms for a warm hug.

"The food made him digivolve," Izzy explained.

Matt clapped his little brother on the shoulder. "Congratulations!"

Tokomon nuzzled into T.K.'s neck. "Together," Tokomon said, "we can make me Patamon again!"

T.K. grinned, feeling thrilled. "Definitely!" he promised.

"Let's hear it for Tokomon!" Mimi cried.

While the friends were celebrating, they failed to notice how unhappy the Pagumon were about Tokomon's transformation. Their orange eyes narrowed and blazed with anger.

But they kept smiling.

8

Late that night, while all the friends slept, the Pagumon sneaked into the top tower room. They grabbed Tokomon and whisked him outside before he could even whimper.

The Pagumon carried Tokomon into the dark woods. "I want my DigiMommy!" Tokomon cried. "Why are you picking on me?"

"Because you digivolved!" a Pagumon replied. The little blobs paused in a moonlit clearing in the forest.

"Fear not, for I am a friend to all," said Gennai.

Poyomon is back . . .

. . . just in time for a whale of a trip to Server!

**Biyomon's infamous Poison Ivy
to the rescue again!**

Drimogemon and Ikkakumon go horn-to-horn.

Mimi and Sora proudly wear their hard-earned tags.

Mimi gets carried away with the mischievous Pagumon.

After a light snack, Poyomon digivolves
to Tokomon . . .

. . . but the Pagumon are none too happy
with his quick change.

Strike a pose, Etemon!

**Etemon's Dark Network Concert Crush
is definitely off-key.**

Tai earns his Crest of Courage!

"What do you think you're doing?" a cruel voice asked.

Tokomon and the Pagumon glanced up to see three punk rabbits standing on their hind legs.

"Oh, no! Gazimon!" Tokomon exclaimed. "On the evil scale of one to ten, ten being the worst . . . Gazimon are twelves!"

The Gazimon who had spoken stepped forward. "Where did that Tokomon come from?" he demanded.

The Pagumon bounced nervously. "He came to our village with some humans, and—"

"There are *humans* here?" the Gazimon leader interrupted. The three nasty rabbits discussed the situation in a huddle. Finally, they decided to let the Pagumon deal with Tokomon before they did anything else. The Gazimon supervised while the Pagumons carried Tokomon farther along the forest trail until they reached a lake. A rippling waterfall cascaded into the pool.

The Pagumon brought Tokomon over to the waterfall. Then the Pagumon ducked *behind* the waterfall, into a secret cave. Inside the dim cave were metal cages. The Pagumon opened one cage and tossed

Tokomon in it, locking him up.

"You're not so special now, are you?" a Pagumon taunted Tokomon.

On a high bluff on the other side of the waterfall, the Gazimon were still discussing what to do. "One of us has to inform Etemon that the human Digidestined are here," the Gazimon leader told his partners.

"I'll go," the shortest rabbit offered. "I have to talk to him about getting time off for a *hare* cut, anyway." He raced away at top speed and quickly covered several miles.

"Where is he?" the vicious bunny fretted as he searched the landscape. He hopped over a rocky plain, heading toward the far coast.

As the sun rose, the short Gazimon reached an abandoned seaside town. "Etemon!" he called, bounding between the crumbling buildings. "Wait until you hear the news I have for you! Where are you, Etemon?"

The Gazimon screeched to a halt when he spotted a huge, bull-like Digimon dragging a cylindrical trailer that looked like a gasoline tank. "Oh, good," the Gazimon said. "Etemon!"

The beast slowed down, and the trailer creaked open. As its lid rose, flashes of disco lights and smoke poured out. Then the smoke cleared, revealing a tall figure holding a microphone. He resembled a giant monkey dressed in an orange jump-suit, and he posed like he was about to start a rock concert. Dark sunglasses covered his eyes. A little doll of Monzaemon hung from his belt.

Etemon smiled, revealing fangs. "Yes, the

concert sensation of the Server Continent is back!" he announced in a cheesy voice. "All right, it's Etemon!"

The short Gazimon bowed. "Everyone hail Etemon, the true king!"

Etemon bopped the Gazimon with his fist. "Son, you're way too loud for an early morning time like this," Etemon rumbled. "You understand?"

The Gazimon stroked his long, furry ears. "But you were the one using the amplifier, sir," he protested.

"Let's get something straight, sonny boy," Etemon snarled in his Southern-fried voice. "*I'm* the monarch of rock and roll. Your job is to make me happy!" He turned to an electronic map of Server that hung in the trailer. A bright blue dot glowed on the ocean, near Server's coast.

"The humans should be here soon," Etemon explained, pointing to the blue dot. "Once I start making my fabulous music . . . well, those kids are going to be mine!" He posed again in a dorky rock star stance.

"They'll just have to come see who's singing—"

"Those seven kids are *already* here," the Gazimon interrupted. "They've been at the Pagumon village since yesterday."

"What?" Etemon hollered. "I had it all worked out, kid! My plan's flawless!"

"Well, somebody forgot to tell those humans," the Gazimon replied.

"It's just not fair!" Etemon screeched. He adjusted the map's controls, and the blue dot shifted to the Pagumon village. "I am the king here! And they'll have to learn that they can't be messing with the royal one! I

expect my plans to be *followed*." Etemon pressed a button on his computer panel. "Launch the Dark Network!"

The bull-like Digimon detached from his yoke and wandered off. Then sinister wires snaked out of the cylindrical trailer. The wires slinked through the abandoned town, slithering across the landscape beyond like black elastic eels.

"Let's go!" Etemon howled. The trailer rumbled into motion. It cruised along the Dark Network's wires like trolley tracks—heading across the hills toward the Pagumon village.

"This will be your greatest performance yet, boss," the Gazimon said.

Etemon chuckled. "It's not easy being a superstar, little bunny," he said. "But somebody's got to do it!"

Back in the village, T.K. wandered between the huts, searching for his missing Digimon. "Tokomon!" he cried miserably. "Where are you?"

Tai stood atop the tall tower, scanning the surrounding area with his spyglass. "Where could he have gone?" he wondered.

On the ground, Sora, Matt, Mimi, and Joe met up in front of the tower door to compare their search efforts. "Well, he's not in the south part of the village," Sora reported.

"Not over to the west, either," Matt added.

Izzy had drawn a map of the area in the dirt. With a stick, he crossed off the places that had already been searched.

The gaggle of Pagumon arrived, giggling. "He's not by the waterfall!" they chirped.

"Okay, thanks," Izzy replied. He drew an **X** over the waterfall on his dirt map. "This is bad," he said.

Every place on his drawing had already been crossed off.

9

Agumon searched for Tokomon deep in the woods. "Something is definitely wrong," he muttered. "My nose always knows." He took a long sniff of the air with his lizard's snout, and his eyes widened. "I smell Koromon!" he exclaimed.

Agumon exited the forest near the lake. He followed the path to the pool's edge, but there the trail ran out. Agumon sniffed

again. "It's coming from behind the water-fall!" he realized.

He hurried into the secret cave.

"Agumon!" Tokomon shouted in greeting.

Agumon gasped as he saw Tokomon locked up in the cage. Then he noticed the dozens of *other* cages. Each had a group of cuddly pale pink blobs trapped in it.

"Koromon!" Agumon exclaimed. "Boy, you guys *have* to get bigger apartments. Maybe something with a few more bed-rooms."

"The Pagumon locked us in these cages!" one Koromon chirped.

"About three days ago they took over our entire village!" another added.

Agumon nodded. "Then we were really right in the first place—"

"Not that I don't appreciate conversation as much as the next guy," Tokomon inter-rupted. "But if you would open this cage, we could warn the others!"

"Right!" Agumon said. He yanked on the cage bars. "I'll have you out in a jiffy—"

"I really don't think so!"

Agumon whirled around and saw two tall rabbitlike Digimon scowling at him. "You're Gazimon!" Agumon cried.

"Exactly right," the Gazimon leader replied. "And we're going to be giving those humans of yours to King Etemon!" His eyes glinted evilly.

Agumon raised his fists. "No, you're *not!*" he declared bravely, narrowing his reptilian eyes.

"Let's teach the little lizard a lesson!" the Gazimon leader yelled. The two punk bunny-like bullies leaped at Agumon, and knocked him to the floor of the cave.

Then they got him while he was down.

Agumon struggled to get up. One of his eyes was swollen badly. He climbed to his feet and glared at the evil bunnylike Digimon.

"Electric Stun Blast!" the Gazimon hollered together. Their eyes glowed with energy. Sizzling beams shot out, combining in the air to form a brilliant ball of power.

The ball slammed into Agumon, and he jittered with electricity. Agumon swayed once. Then he fell onto his face.

"Two against one isn't fair!" Tokomon protested.

Agumon raised his head weakly. "Tai!" he shouted. "Please come and help me digivolve—!"

"Go ahead, yell if you want," the Gazimon sneered. "Your friend can't hear you." The sound of tumbling water blocked out all other noises.

"If only it weren't for this waterfall," Agumon moaned. Then he perked up slightly. "That's it!"

Agumon lifted himself up on his arms and inhaled deeply. "Pepper Breath!" he hollered, spitting out a compact ball of flame.

The Gazimon hopped out of the way. The blast of fire sizzled into the curtain of rippling water. A section of the waterfall boiled briefly.

Outside the cave, a puff of steam rose into the air.

"Pepper Breath!" Agumon yelled again, blasting another steam puff out of the falls. "Pepper Breath!"

The Gazimon watched from the side, confused. "What are you trying to do, you dolt?" one asked.

Agumon's only answer was another fireball. "Pepper Breath!"

Tai searched the forest with his spyglass from the top of the village tower. "Agumon's been gone a long time," he muttered to himself. "I wonder if he's found anything—" Tai suddenly spotted a steam signal billowing over the trees. "That's odd," he said loudly.

"What do you see, Tai?" Matt called from the ground below.

"Smoke by the river!" Tai shouted back.

T.K. let out a big cheer. "It's Tokomon!"

The Pagumon swarmed around the kids' feet. "No, really, it's nothing!" one chirped. "We already looked by the waterfall and didn't see a thing!"

"Well," Izzy suggested, rubbing his chin, "it is possible that Tokomon arrived after you Pagumon searched the area."

Tai hurried down the tower stairs and rushed out the front door. "I'll check it out!" he declared.

"No," the Pagumon squealed. "Don't do that! Just take our word for it!"

A nearby scream from Mimi grabbed everyone's attention. "Ew!" she cried. "What is this thing?" Mimi sat on a bench with what looked like a smiling cat's head in her lap. Palmon stood nearby, watching warily.

Tentomon buzzed over for a better look. "It's a Botamon!" he announced. "Botamon are the small egg forms that digivolve into

Koromon, and then into Agumon!"

"But this is a Pagumon village," Palmon said. "Why would there be a Botamon here?"

Tai crossed his arms over his chest. "Because the Pagumon lied to us."

The Pagumon bounced away, heading out of the village. As they departed, they sang.

It's time for us to leave here.
We really hate to go.
We told you this was our place . . .
now you know it isn't so.

Pagumon is our name.
We're clever and we're bright.
You can tell we're smart because
we'd rather run than fight!

"There they go," Sora said as she watched the pack vanish around a corner.

"Never trust anything without feet," Tai added. Then he pushed the Pagumon out of his mind. "C'mon!" he shouted. "Let's go get Tokomon!"

* * *

Inside the secret cave, the Gazimon picked up Agumon by his arms. Then they pushed him against the rock wall. Agumon grunted in pain and fell backward, between the mean bunnylike Digimon's big feet.

"Agumon–!" Tokomon cried. He pressed worriedly against his cage bars.

The two Gazimon glared down at the hurt reptile. "Get ready, lizard!" the leader taunted. He pulled back his fist to wallop Agumon again.

Agumon tried to lift his head, but he was too hurt. "Tai, where are you?" he moaned sadly, closing his eyes.

10

"Agumon!" shouted a voice on the other side of the waterfall.

Popping open his eyes, Agumon struggled to push himself up. "Tai, here I am!" he yelled with the last of his strength. "Help me!"

Tai rushed around the waterfall, barreling into the cave. "Agumon, hold on!" he hollered. "Are you okay?"

Agumon smiled. "Now I am!" he replied.

The Gazimon leader gazed menacingly at Tai. "So, you're one of the Digidestined!" he sneered.

Tai ignored the vile Digimon. "Digivolving time!" he called to Agumon.

"You got it!" the little lizardlike Digimon bellowed. "Agumon digivolve to . . . Greymon!" Instantly, the cave was filled with scintillating digital information. Agumon exploded with power as he transformed into a tall triceratops with tiger stripes along his body. A fearsome black mask covered his face and sharp horns.

Greymon roared at the Gazimon, and they shrank back in fear. Then the Champion reached up and shifted a few boulders on top of the waterfall. The sheet of cascading liquid parted like a curtain, opening the cave to the outside.

By the pond, the other kids and Digimon cheered as they saw Greymon taking control.

"So, you like to fight two against one, eh?" Greymon thundered at the punk Gazimon. "Nova Blast!" A gigantic fireball blazed out of the digivolved Digimon's mouth. It slammed into the Gazimon and blasted them backward into the river.

"Help!" the Gazimon leader cried. "I can't swim!" The mean bunnylike Digimon coughed and spluttered as the strong river rapids swept them downstream.

"Greymon did it!" Tai cheered.

T.K. hurried into the cave and yanked open Tokomon's cage. "I thought I'd lost you again!" T.K. whimpered.

Tokomon nuzzled T.K.'s cheek. "I'm like a boomerang," he assured his friend. "I keep coming back."

Sora, Joe, Izzy, and Mimi helped the others free the Koromon. "The Pagumon are gone," Sora told the baby Digimon. "You can all return to your village now!"

"Thank you!" the Koromon squeaked as they hopped out of the tight cages. "You saved us!"

"Ah, hello!" a rumbling voice boomed from outside the cave. All the kids and the Digimon turned to look. They saw a giant fanged monkey in a purple jumpsuit looking down at them over a wall of trees. He was twice as tall as Greymon. His sunglasses glinted in the sunlight, and his microphone squawked from feedback.

"Oh, great," Joe groaned. "A Digi–Rock Star!"

"You measly little Digidestined humans, hello!" the dorky monkey bellowed.

"It's Etemon!" a Koromon gasped in fear. "It's the king!"

Etemon twanged his guitar. "Thank you very much," he drawled. "You little bratty kids messed up my big beautiful plan. So now I'm going to punish y'all by playing a little number I just wrote. It's called, 'Wrecking the Whole Place.'"

"Wrecking the Whole Place?" Tai repeated. That didn't sound like a good tune.

"Dark Network Concert Crush!" Etemon hollered.

The entire village shook. Cracks jagged across the ground between the huts. The cracks shimmered with electricity, turned black, and then slowly levitated into the air.

All the zigzags connected to form a mesh of dark lines like a net.

Etemon yowled with howls of laughter.

Red streaks of power sizzled across the net, zapping scarlet bolts down at the little huts. Each building that was touched by the grid disintegrated instantly. The tall tower was the first to get fried.

The Koromon screamed in terror as their village was destroyed.

"Everyone, digivolve now!" Sora ordered.

Gabumon ran forward to stand next to Greymon. "Gabumon digivolve to . . .

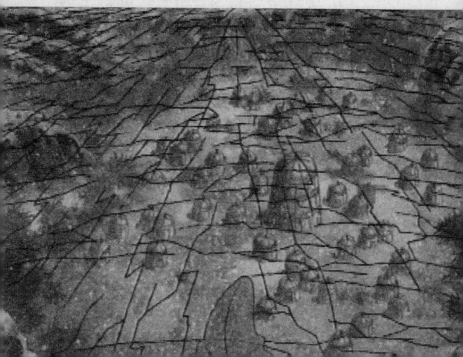

Garurumon!" the furry hamsterlike Digimon hollered.

In a blazing whirlwind of intense digital energy, Gabumon transformed into what looked like a zebra-striped giant tiger with eagle's feathers.

Garurumon roared as he leaped at the monkey musician.

Etemon didn't look worried at all. "Well, you say you want a digivolution?" he sang. He strummed his ill-tuned guitar. "Guess what, the answer's no! Dark Network Concert Crush!"

In response to Etemon's awful music, the network lines crackled with power. The grid spread for miles in every direction.

"Gotcha, baby!" Etemon crowed.

As the network flashed, Garurumon and Greymon screamed. The twisted energy forced them to painfully shrink back to their rookie forms.

"Dark Network, yeah!" Etemon cheered. He raised his guitar above his head and awkwardly danced around. Meanwhile, his evil grid was still zapping huts in the Tokomon's village.

Agumon and Gabumon collapsed to the cave floor, twitching in agony. "Concert Crush took our power!" Agumon cried.

"Does rock and roll have that effect in your world?" Tentomon asked the kids.

"Only on our parents," Sora replied.

Izzy turned to Tentomon. "So there's no way for us to fight this monster?"

"As we are, no," Tentomon said. "If only we could digivolve a step further—"

"Run, run!" the Koromon called. They hopped deeper into the cave. "Get away!"

Etemon squawked his guitar, and a network zap hit the mouth of the cave. The boulders on top of the waterfall crumbled, tumbling toward the friends.

The kids and the Digimon rushed to follow the Koromon farther inside. The avalanche just missed burying them under heavy stones.

But the rocks blocked off the exit to the lake.

The friends raced after the Koromon through long, dark tunnels with cut stone walls. Finally, the Koromon led the group to a dead end, where they stopped.

"What's this?" Tai asked.

The Koromon closest to Tai hopped up and down. "This is a safe place where we hide when anything bad happens to the village."

Tai glanced around the narrow rectangular room. "What do we do now?"

Suddenly, the tags began to glow on the chains around all the kids' necks. The walls of the stone room flashed orange. They grew brighter by the second.

"What—?" Tai exclaimed.

Strange swirling symbols appeared on the walls, flashing and changing shape. A giant sunburst symbol flashed on the dead end next to Tai, and that wall remained glowing after the side walls faded back to stone. A rectangle of brilliant light pulled free from the dead end and warped into a thin sheet of shining orange energy. Then it shrank to the size of a credit card.

Tai gasped in amazement as the card glided through the air and slid into a slot on his tag. It settled, dangling around Tai's neck, sunburst side up.

"I think I know what this is!" Tai exclaimed.

Matt stared at him skeptically. "Okay, what?" he asked.

"A crest," Tai replied.

Everybody murmured in awe.

Agumon peered at the symbol inside Tai's tag. "It's the Crest of Courage," he whispered respectfully.

"Awesome," Matt breathed.

Sora pointed to the dead end wall, which was still glowing brightly. "Hey, look!" she called. As it got brighter, the wall became more and more transparent, until it vanished entirely.

Through the open space, the friends could see a lush, peaceful forest with a blue sky above it. There was no sign of Etemon—or any of his nasty hench-Digimon.

"Wasn't there just a wall here?" Joe asked as he stared at the mountains covered with evergreen trees in the distance.

"Yes," a Koromon answered Joe. "But the crest must have transported us here! Those mountains are a long way from our village."

"All right!" Joe cheered. "Frequent flyer miles!"

Mimi beamed happily at the view. "It's beautiful," she sighed.

Tai held his tag and studied the new crest. "With this, we can do anything we want," he said. "You know, guys, I think this is the first step on our trip home!"

Unseen by any of the friends, something moved in the bushes a few feet away. A Dark Network wire raised up out of the underbrush, and a blip of crimson information zipped along it.

Back at the flattened Koromon village, Etemon howled with laughter as the information reached him through the wire.

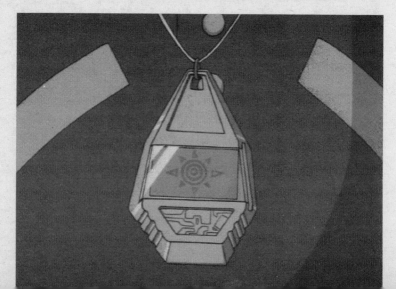

He'd be able to track down the Digi-destined humans in no time at all.

Write Your Own Digimon Story!

Fill out the blank spaces according to the cues given below. On the following page, your answers will be used to create a story about your own adventure in Digi-World. Don't look at the story on the next page yet, because that will spoil the fun of seeing your hilarious story before it's finished.

1. A silly name: _____.
2. Name of a town: _____.
3. Name of a game or sport: _____.
4. Name of your best friend: _____.
5. A color: _____.
6. A natural disaster (example: "tornado"):

_____.
7. A foreign country: _____.
8. Your favorite Digimon character from Season 2:

_____.
9. An enthusiastic, silly greeting (example: "Whazzup!"): _____.
10. A noun (A noun is a person, place, or thing, like, "rock"): _____.
11. Another noun: _____.

12. A type of weather (example: "rainy"): _____.

13. A noun: _____.

14. Type of animal: _____.

15. Name of a scary Digimon: _____.

16. Body part (example: "arm"): _____.

17. A noun: _____.

18. A body of water (example: "lake"): _____.

19. An emotion (examples: "happy" or "confused"):

_____.

20. A noun: _____.

21. Type of clothing: _____.

22. An exclamation (example: "Look out!"): _____.

23. A noun: _____.

24. Your school: _____.

My Day in DigiWorld
By _____
1.

You'll never believe what happened to me. I was

hanging out one summer day in _____,

2.

playing _____ with _____ .

3.   4.

All of a sudden, the sky turned _____ and a

5.

huge _____ hit and carried us off to

6.

DigiWorld. I thought we were in _____ until I
                                              7.
saw _____ . He came up and said,
          8
"_____."
          9.

   We started walking through DigiWorld, checking out

all the Digi-_____ and Digi-_____. It
                    10.   11.
was really _____ outside, so we decided to just
                    12.
play around and throw _____(s) at each other.
                              13.

   But just when I forgot about my pet _____
                                                      14.
back home and started thinking I would stay in

DigiWorld forever, _____ showed up. He
                          15.
growled at us and showed us his terrible

_____ . He used his scary Digi-_____
        16.   17.
against us, pushing us slowly toward the _____ .
                                                  18.
That's when I really started to feel _____ ,
                                              19.
because I can't swim! We had to do something quick.

   Luckily, with the help of the Crest of Knowledge

93

and the Digi-egg of _____, the tide of the battle

20.

started to change. I noticed the digivice attached to my

_____, and I used it to help my Digimon

21.

friend digivolve. Then I yelled, "_____," to

22.

distract the enemy, and all three of us started kicking

some Digi-Butt! Finally, our evil Digimon opponent

gave up and ran away.

Our adventure was over and it was time for me

to go home. I told my new friend he was a real

_____ , and that he should come visit

23.

me some time. I sure hope that he does, because I

want to show him off to my friends at _____.

24.